The Super Twins

Andy Slinger

Twin Dad Ltd

First paperback edition March 2021

Book design by Andy Slinger
Illustrations by Kate Mottershaw
Edited by Kirsty Ridge

ISBN (paperback) 978-1-8381013-0-5
ISBN (ebook) 978-1-8381013-1-2
Published by Twin Dad Ltd
www.andyslinger.com

Dedicated to:

The real-life Super Twins Luke and Liam who
have inspired me every day to finish this book.

Chapter One

Torrential rain bounced on the roof of the car; the windscreen wipers swished on overdrive. Jake was sure at any moment they would fly off into the dark woodland that flanked either side of the road, as Ryan slept soundly beside him. How he could sleep through this Jake couldn't fathom out: their connection only seemed to function in waking hours. He wished Ryan would wake up to share this burden – he couldn't cope without him. He needed his best friend to annoy, poke, make fun of and laugh at, despite the fact that the glint in his eye had vanished. Jake felt numb, lonelier than he had ever felt in his life.

The death of their mother had hit them both hard. A sudden heart attack had shocked the family deeply and the boys were now lost. Doctors said the warning signs had been there: the high cholesterol, the lack of exercise, the junk food and the excessive drinking had all contributed to her demise. Jake wondered what he could have done to stop it happening. They had pretty much fended for themselves as she had never really been there for them, so their focus had been on survival.

As a result, everything had suffered: they were failing at school, had a bad diet, were dirty, unkempt and lucky to have one bath a month between them. They did have each other, though, and that had got them through life up to now. They could always rely on one another. The twins had a wicked sense of humour, constantly pranking just about anybody and regularly pretending to be one another, to keep everyone guessing. Even so, they hated it when people got their names wrong when they weren't playing a practical joke.

Despite the fact they were identical, they couldn't have been more like chalk and cheese in terms of personality. Ryan was the thinker, and loved to mull over schemes and consider ideas. He often provided moments of genius. Jake, on the other hand, was a real live wire. He was sporty and confident to the point of being cocky. He was the brawn to Ryan's brains.

In terms of looks, there was very little to separate them, aside from Jake having a dimple when he smiled. They both had longish, straw-like, scraggly brown hair and dazzling blue eyes. They were so slim they were verging on malnutrition – that's what years of missing meals had done to them. They had thick lips and a cheeky smile that had enabled them to get away with murder.

Although they had such different personalities, they had three things in common. They hated vegetables with a passion: anything green was a massive no-no. Ryan once got detention for flooding the school toilets with a concoction of broccoli and Brussel sprouts. Alongside this, they could never understand why after spending their whole day at school they should have to work in the evenings too, and consequently hated any form of homework. Not that either of them ever bothered to do their homework anyway. Their final bugbear was early nights. They had always been used to going to bed at whatever time they wanted to as Mum had never bothered. Most of the time she wasn't there to enforce it, even if she did care.

The only time they had to face these problems, though, was when they spent the weekend at their dad's. He was a tall, well-built man in his mid-forties, with a strong jaw, bald head and a constant stern expression that had etched permanent lines in his forehead over the years. He was incredibly strict: everything was to a schedule and done with precision. From 5:00pm till 6:00pm: Reading, 6:00pm till 7:00pm: Maths. Dad's house was such a well-oiled machine, he even forced them to bath. It was the only time they ever did! He was a true man's man after his time in the military had taught him how to hide his emotions, yet the boys knew he loved them to bits.

Yet here they were on the long journey from their Grandma's to spend the rest of their lives with their dad. How were they going to cope?! They both knew he loved them dearly, but to live over at his pokey, minimalist semi-detached house, with the only picture on his wall a schedule of jobs, was going to be tough.

As Grandma pulled up outside the house and mounted the curb in the process, Jake wondered if this was how criminals felt when they arrived outside prison for a life sentence. At least they had their uncle's farm and their grandma's to escape to. Dad was standing to attention, bolt upright at the front door, tapping on his watch, staring straight ahead, a slight smirk forming in the corner of his mouth. He knew that life would never be the same again: it was all one big nightmare. He gave Ryan a quick jab in the ribs, which woke him up with a grunt and a splutter.

"We're here! Prepare yourself and look like you're awake," Jake announced.

Chapter Two

Later that evening they were all sitting down in the living room watching TV. Dad loved having the boys at home with him; perhaps now he could provide them with the life they deserved. He wanted to show them he cared, and he wanted them to grow up to have healthy and happy lives. They had been through too much for boys their age and now it was all down to him to bring them up the right way. A regular routine, healthy eating and exercise would pay dividends in the long run. He felt bad they had been left isolated from everything they had known.

"Jake, I've got a treat for you tonight. Run to the fridge and grab the spinach dip and carrot pieces will you, lad."

Jake begrudgingly peeled himself off his seat, dragging his feet to the kitchen while muttering a few inaudible grunts.

"Ryan, do me a favour and drag that coffee table into the middle of the room. I've a new board game for us to play."

Ryan rolled his eyes and did as he was asked. Dad would soon get the boys up to speed; he had to keep reminding himself to go easy on them for now. In the army they'd never have been so soft on him, and that had made him the man he was today, but he had to remember they were only 13.

As Ryan slumped back down into his seat, a loud *crack* from the direction of the kitchen made him jump straight back up in the air. Dad exploded into fits of laughter as Jake stormed past, hair sticking up like a porcupine, and ran upstairs.

"That was NOT funny!" he screamed as the bedroom door slammed shut.

"What did you do?" laughed Ryan, who'd seen the funny side to the prank.

"I just wired the fridge door up with some bangers – nothing dangerous, just tiny fireworks. An old trick I learned in the forces." He chuckled as he spoke.

"I'd best go check he's OK. I can hear the weights clanging around already; he'll end up coming through the ceiling at this rate."

Upstairs, Ryan approached his brother with caution as he watched him swinging weights around his head like someone possessed.

"He was only trying to lighten the mood, you know – that's just his humour. Surely you can see the funny side of it; it's not like we don't prank people a lot ourselves."

"Our pranks are different: they're not as bad. And it's always me that takes the brunt of his practical jokes!"

Jake continued to throw the weights up and down, his face redder than a genetically modified tomato on steroids.

"I just think you should tone down the anger a bit, bro. He's trying his best despite the circumstances." He was sprawled out on his bed, book in hand as usual.

"Easy for you to say!" Jake threw his weights down in the corner of the room with a soft thud.

Booooom!

CRASH! The windows exploded in around them and Ryan was thrown off his bed. He landed with his feet sticking up in the air. He saw Jake's face smash straight into the solid pine bookshelf and heard an ominous creaking sound, as the shelving unit collapsed around him. The ground shook for what felt like a whole minute but was probably nearer ten seconds, as the house groaned and rasped. A huge crack appeared from the bottom to the top of the wall.

"What the hell was that?" yelled Ryan as he inched away from the wall, towards his brother.

"An earthquake?" Jake's voice trembled as the words left his lips, unsure what on earth had happened. His nostrils filled with cement dust as he tried to right himself, soon realising that he was unable to move a muscle. The crack shifted up and across the ceiling before an almighty groan and the ceiling came down around them. They were plunged into blackness.

Chapter Three

Jake woke to a bright light shining into his eyes.
"Jake... Jake can you hear me?" the voice of an angel
sang in his ear; his body ached all over. He looked
around him: he was in a small hospital room hooked up
to various machines, an intravenous drip inserted into
his arm. A plump nurse with curly hair and coffee-
stained teeth stood in front of him, adjusting the
position of his bed with her chubby foot. She definitely
sounded better than she looked, thought Jake.

"Am I dead? How did I get here? Where is Ryan?"
He was distressed and confused. The last thing he
remembered was opening the fridge and the door
exploding in his face, and the next he was here. What
had happened? Oh yeah, hang on ... the explosion, the

crashes all around him. The fog in his mind began to lift a little.

"Did we get attacked? Was that a bomb?" he stuttered, staring at the round mass that was the nurse. "How long have I been here?"

"Nooo, something far cooler than that!"

Jake jerked his head to the side to see the familiar face of his twin smiling from ear to ear.

"It was a freaking asteroid!" Ryan couldn't spit the words out fast enough. "It landed smash, bang in the middle of our garden, taking half the house with it! We were lucky to get out alive. You've been in here weeks; we didn't think you were going to make it at one point! Me and Dad have been visiting you every day; he's determined to get you out of here."

The nurse stepped in and intervened. "Right, that's enough for now. The poor boy has only just regained consciousness." Jake thought he would be knocked out again if she got any closer with that horrendous breath.

"Just lie back, Jake, you've had a nasty bang to the head. You need to stay still and rest. Too much excitement is the last thing you need right now."

Jake reached his hand to his head, where a bandage met his touch: he must have been extremely lucky. He felt no pain whatsoever, in fact why was the bandage even there? It was as though he'd had a long and tranquil sleep: he was feeling refreshed, rejuvenated, revitalised.

Ryan waited for the gigantic nurse to depart and slid a copy of the local *Echo* over to Jake. The front page read: *"Attack of the Asteroid?"*

The cover picture was of their garden, or rather what was left of it. There was a huge crater, into which a massive asteroid as tall as their house had wedged itself. There was a strange green glow about it. Men in white suits were scattered around the perimeter, holding a range of wacky and wonderful instruments. The back wall of the house was no longer in existence; you could see right inside their room, the remains of the toilet, the back of the kitchen and the living room.

"Oh my God, what's happened to Dad? Is he OK?" Jake had a note of urgency in his voice.

"Erm … he's OK, although he isn't himself at the moment. The doctors are saying it's shock but I'm not so sure. I'm sure it won't be too long before he's here to see you; he popped out for some air not long ago. We have got sick of these four walls and cramped chairs. I'm sure he'll be as delighted as I am to see that you're OK." Ryan grinned as he pulled a small screen over the bed. "It's been weeks since the meteorite, and our house is still all that's on the TV."

On the news there was aerial footage of their house, with a large military presence. The local reporter was interviewing an officer called Adiran Gedeon, saying anyone trying to gain access to the area would be shot on sight. He had a sinister glint in his eye as he said the words and Jake felt that he was the type of guy to go around shooting people for fun.

Just then the door flew open and standing in the doorway was their dad. He wore a strained expression on his face, his forehead a ploughed field, his eyes dark and disturbed. The stress of recent events had clearly got to him: it was like he hadn't slept in weeks and was ready to drop at any second.

"Jake! You're awake at last, thank goodness! How are you feeling?" Dad looked concerned as he spoke.

"I'm fine. I feel like I've had the best sleep of my life; I feel on top of the world!" Jake sat up and stretched his arms up high, before unravelling the bandage from his head.

"Should you really be doing that? Aren't you in pain? You've been unconscious for weeks, son. We've been back and forth from the temporary house, visiting you every day. It was only yesterday that the nurses got any sort of response from you, so you can't expect to jump up and leave just like that."

"There is nothing wrong with me! Who says we can't get out of here now? That nurse isn't even here any more! If I start to feel worse, you can always bring me back. I feel more alive than I ever have in my life."

Dad paused for a moment, considering Jake's point of view, before a devious smile appeared on his lips.

"Give me a minute, lad — I'll see what I can do. Ryan and I have been waiting for this moment. It's not been the same without you." He edged over to the door and began talking to the police guards outside. The boys could see Dad's arms waving around but couldn't quite make out what was being said despite their best attempts. After five minutes of heated discussion the door swung open again.

"We are leaving, right now," stated Dad urgently. "The police are going to sneak us out of the back door of this place, before anyone realises that you're awake. Reporters are swarming around the building like flies round…"

His voice trailed off as three police officers walked through the swinging doors. Two bulky officers, menacing looking, one with a spiral tattoo on his right hand, either side of a tall skinny man in a suit, who had the look of authority.

"Are you ready now, Mr Rutherford?" the thin man began as Dad nodded.

"Make your way with us right now. We don't have long to get out of here before the reporters catch wind of this and all hell breaks loose."

Ryan raised himself up out of the uncomfortable hospital chair, moving across to give Jake a hand out of bed.

"Put your arm over my shoulder and I'll help you up."

"I don't need your help – there is nothing wrong with me." Jake laughed as he launched himself up and out of the bed, grabbing an apple off the bedside table which he crushed into bits of pulp, juice and seeds with two fingers. "Whoops … I hardly touched that."

Ryan's jaw dropped as he stared at his twin in complete disbelief.

Chapter Four

Later that evening Jake and Ryan were lying on their pop-up beds, in their make-do room; Jake was staring up at the ceiling, still feeling fresh as a daisy. Ryan was glaring moodily at his phone, his elation at the hospital having evaporated since arriving here.

"Do you notice something different?" Jake probed.

"How do you mean?" replied Ryan sharply. "Maybe the fact that our mum has died, our dad is acting extremely weird, or possibly because our house has been struck by a meteorite and is lying in ruins. You could say that something is different!"

"No, you plank!" retorted Jake. "I mean in how you feel, since the meteorite?"

"Yeah, I feel very different. I feel like my life is over and I've lost everything. My mind is running a million miles an hour," snapped Ryan.

Jake propped himself up on his elbow, staring at the plaster flaking off the wall next to him.

"I don't mean mentally, I mean physically. Since the accident I feel ... stronger, more powerful, like nothing could stop me!"

"More powerful – what are you on about? Our lives get tipped upside down, almost beyond repair, and all you can think is that you feel powerful? You're nuts!" Ryan laughed with astonishment at Jake's comments.

"Really, though, I noticed it on the way out of the hospital. I went to tie my shoelaces and they just snapped off in my hand. Then when I pushed the door open it nearly swung off its hinges but I hardly even touched it!" He could see that his brother really wasn't taking him seriously at all.

Ryan burst into rapturous laughter. "Whooaaa, Jake the powerful, Jake the wondrous, the destroyer of men. He rips apart rotten shoelaces with his bare hands – what a legend. I wish I had that incredible power!" the sarcasm came in full flow.

Jake's eyes narrowed threateningly; he clenched his fists, cracking his knuckles.

"No, stop right there and listen to me: that was just the start. I tried to flush the toilet and the handle came straight off in my hand, then when the hand drier wouldn't work, I gave it a bash to get it working and it went flying across the room. There were bits of metal everywhere. I can't control my own strength."

He paused, took a breath and then continued: "I know I'm upset; I know I'm angry, and I know these aren't normal circumstances, but there has been a massive change in me. I am stronger than I've ever been, not just a little bit stronger but ten times stronger.

I know you saw me grab that apple at the hospital and crush it with one hand." His voice trailed off as he looked across at his twin.

Ryan's face contorted as the penny dropped.

"Oh my… Yes, the apple!"

Ryan's mind began racing faster than it had ever done before. A visual map of the many events appeared in his mind and in a thousandth of a second he had connected the many dots. He was streets ahead of his brother, who just stared at him with a blank expression.

"Do you realise what has happened? That asteroid, the scientists, the green aura, the police, taking parts of the rock for testing. It doesn't take a brain scientist to work it all out. It's no coincidence that we come into contact with a radioactive asteroid one minute and the next you have the power to a crush fruit with two fingers."

"But what about you? Surely there has been some change to you. It can't just be me that's developed powers." Jake was starting to ask the right questions.

"Well, at the moment of impact you were exercising and all of a sudden you've developed more strength. Meanwhile I was reading that book and I know there has been an improvement in my IQ. Everything seems so much clearer to me; I'm more focussed, alive, quicker, sharper, more enhanced mentally."

"You still look just as stupid to me," laughed Jake.

Ryan looked at his brother, puzzled about what it must be like inside his head.

"You wouldn't notice superior intelligence if it smacked you right in the face. You were never blessed with brains – that was always my gift in this twin partnership." As he spoke, he contemplated how much easier life must be when you had a satsuma-sized brain.

"No need for that, I have brains: I'm just stronger, fitter and sportier than you are; I always have been. And now, now we have turned into superheroes!"

"No, bonehead, it's improved our capabilities. It's fine-tuned our talents, massively improved our proficiency at whatever we were doing at the point of impact. This doesn't make us superheroes, it has just changed us … for the better," Ryan said smugly as a wry smile formed on his dry, cracked lips.

"But this does make us special! There is no reason we couldn't use our powers." Jake leapt off his bed. "You do know what this means, don't you?"

"Of course I know what this means: I was the one who told you what has happened. And be quiet. Jump around like that and you're going to wake Dad! We have to keep all this quiet, even from Dad. If anyone hears about this, it will be us being taken away for medical research not just lumps of meteorite rock." Ryan's tone had changed: he was deadly serious and his jawline tensed as he spoke clearly and slowly.

"We have to swear that no one will ever find out about this!"

Jake had a look of doubt written across his face, or maybe it was that his brain was slowly trying to catch up.

"OK, OK, I get your point! But we have to make the most of this. I mean, it's not every day you wind up in a freak accident and end up with superpowers," Jake exclaimed. Ryan could sense a lack of sincerity in his answer.

"You're not listening to me, Jake. We have to swear an oath of secrecy, here and now. Not a soul can find out about this. It has the potential to ruin our lives more than they already are. How we use our powers is our joint decision and is something we need to think long and hard about. We need to swear down on our mum's grave that this stays between us," Ryan's expression was stern.

"Yes, yes, yes, OK, OK, I swear: I won't tell a soul without your permission. But I do have a condition – well, several conditions. This is a gift we have been given and we should use it wisely," Jake pondered as he spoke...

"We can help the world if we choose to. We shouldn't use this to our own advantage but for the greater good. If we really think about this, we can be something amazing. Think about it... Superbikes, a cool base, costumes, capes, weapons, top-of-the-range tech: the sky is the limit." Jake was getting excited, bouncing around between the beds.

"Stop right there! Have you even thought for a second about the practicalities of all this? It's not like you're Bruce Wayne sitting on billions of dollars; we have barely got three quid between us. We have nowhere for a base, not even basic sewing skills to make a suit, and neither of us is even close to the age where we can drive, never mind a Superbike!" As Ryan spoke, his mind remained calm. He had already formulated his plan. He knew exactly what the next step was; in fact, he knew what the next ten steps were. He just had to keep his brother grounded. He knew that Jake was the biggest threat to the Super Twins, so he had to manage his impulsiveness carefully.

Chapter Five

Ryan's eyes opened, immediately focussed on his alarm clock: 5:00am. It was time to take action. He leapt out of bed and headed with purpose straight to the little white desk in the corner of the room, grabbing the battered old laptop his mother had left him. It still had the remains of a worn heart sticker stuck on the front which he had seen his mother's fingers brush over a thousand times. He would never remove that sticker, no matter how tatty and girly it was: it had deep meaning for him. It reminded him of the only memorable and intimate occasions he had spent with his mum, sitting on the shabby, cracked leather sofa, watching stupid videos on this laptop and laughing.

Now, though, things were very different, and he had to focus. He had a vision which had to be realised and time was of the essence; now he could make her proud. His fingers danced over the laptop keys, pausing only to pull a stray piece of fluff from under the letter Q and then to wipe a smear from the screen which was obscuring a vital piece of his plan from his line of sight.

Ryan's fingers were now moving ferociously around the keyboard, extremely detailed graphs, diagrams, drawings, pie and Gantt charts popping up all over the screen. It all amalgamated into a highly detailed report, a plan of action that covered every eventuality. At the bottom of each section appeared a guide (an idiot's guide) for Jake which broke down the basic points in simpler terms. He glanced at the clock in the bottom corner of his screen which read 5:11am – nearly done. Just the finishing touches to complete and we can get started, he thought.

At 5:13am Ryan decided it was time to put the plan into action. He moved over and gently shook his twin.

"Wake up, wake up, lazy bones: it's time."

"What … what's going on? What time is it?"

"It's 5:15: time to get started."

"Are you actually insane … 5:15 in the morning? What plan? What is specifically wrong with you?"

"Get your bum out of bed; we need to get started NOW. You wanted us to use our powers for good… Well, I have worked out exactly how: we are going to become superheroes…" He yanked the curtains back from the single-paned windows as the first bright beams of sunlight streaked into the room. Any thoughts of time vanished from Jake's mind and he jumped to his feet.

"Tell me everything. I want to know it all!"

Ryan proceeded to run through every last detail of his master plan, multiple times until it sank into Jake's brain. He covered every aspect from sourcing materials, to building their headquarters, tracking devices, training, costumes, transport, strategies, battle plans and he'd even given them a superhero name.

"Wonder Twins! Are you kidding me? If you think we are going to be called that then you have something coming to you!" Jake was outraged.

"You put together this huge scientific plan and then don't even come up with a half-decent name! It sounds like some terrible superhero comic from 1977. I can imagine it now: Wonder Twin, power-activate!"

"Well, I don't see you doing anything to help. What's your big idea, Einstein?" Ryan quipped.

"OK then, what about Power Twins? Imagine us fighting our arch-rivals, my power punch saving the day, while you sit down and read a book!"

"That's worse than mine," laughed Ryan. "Without my big brains there would be no super anything. Let's come back to this: there are more pressing matters at hand. We need to start at the beginning. Constructing our base is the most important thing for now as it clearly states on Page 3 of the plan. This will give us time and space to pull together all the other aspects in secret."

Ryan began to talk through how they could expand the den on their uncle's farm, using their existing area as a cover for the high-tech base. The boys quite often spent time up there, using old tractor tyres and pallets to create a lair. Their uncle just left them to it so they wouldn't be disturbed. He was usually too busy searching for lost sheep in the hills or milking his cows to be concerned with what they were up to.

What they had in abundance there on the farm was raw materials: a whole field filled with old tractor parts, machinery, broken gates and piles of rubble was exactly what they needed. It had been sitting there for years rotting, rusting and becoming concealed by the long grass growing in between the items.

Ryan had worked out that all they needed to do was conceal the entrance with pallets and a tarpaulin so they could dig into the base of the hill and create a cavity big enough to house their equipment. They could prop the inside up with old timber, use corrugated iron for the walls and Ryan could fix a battered old generator to give them much-needed electricity to power their headquarters. With time they could expand the place, making improvements in tech, developing a home away from home.

Jake showed great enthusiasm for the plan but hadn't quite clicked that the majority of the work was going to be down to him and his super strength. Ryan had calculated that a couple of hours of intense work was all they would need and the main shell of the construction would be complete. It was time to get cracking.

***

At Phelps Farm, Jake had been working hard. As he forced the final girder into place, the shell of their base was complete. At first glance, Ryan thought it looked more like a room leading off a First World War trench than a superhero base but that was beside the point. This was somewhere they could get away from everything, work on their plans and build their weapons and gadgets in peace. The room stretched ten metres in radius: a large circular chamber with a solid tree trunk beam carved into shape in the centre. Struts came off this beam at angles, creating a sturdy, fan-shaped ceiling. Wooden slabs curved round the base of the central column in a full circle to form Ryan's workbenches.

Ryan had laid out a variety of salvaged electrical components, machinery and various tools which he had 'acquired' from Dad's toolbox. Various half-built devices and weapons were stored under the desks along with an old tractor engine that was to be used as a generator. When he yanked the chain, it spluttered, coughed and fired into life, and they had light. The place needed a lot of sprucing up but it was spacious if nothing else. Phase one was well under way.

"We could sure do with Grandma's decorating skills in here; she would definitely make it more homely," remarked Jake.

"We can hardly bring her down here, now, can we dude? 'Oh come on, Grandma, do you mind just coming and decorating our secret superhero base?'" Ryan chuckled to himself. "There is something we can get her to do, though, and she'd never remember that she'd done it afterwards."

Their grandma was a lovely old lady, often found lost in the local corner shop buying just another slab of carrot cake. She had started to lose her marbles long ago but had the biggest heart, a long-standing passion for arts and crafts and obviously tea and cake.

She was an extremely talented sewing machinist, so Ryan had already decided to give plans to her of their outfits. He was sure she'd be happy to make them. He could pretend it was a top-secret school project they were working on before starting back at school; she would be none the wiser. If he gave her the plans that evening, they would have their outfits ready by the end of the week, provided he gave her a little reminder every day.

Little did his brother know that he'd already decided on a name for the pair. The Super Twins had been born...

Chapter Six

Since the asteroid incident there had been some strange goings-on in the sleepy town of Trincaster. Most residents had put it down to the reduced police presence on the streets and the latest government in power. This coupled with the influx of 'outsiders' on the new housing development had been a cause for concern. It had popped up on the outskirts of the town despite huge protests. Many had said it had brought a bad sort to the town.

Ryan analysed the evidence and felt the truth of the matter was that something more sinister was afoot. It was no coincidence that on almost a daily basis a serious crime was being committed with zero evidence being left at any of the crime scenes and no witnesses. The local fast-food joint had been burnt to the ground, the amusement arcade had all of its electrical wiring removed without so much as a stray hair left at the scene, and all the pins at the bowling alley had miraculously vanished, while it was still open.

He was convinced this had to be the work of a professional despite the strange choice of targets and seemingly no connection between the illegal acts. The local police force was baffled: the biggest crime they had to solve before the last few weeks was the mysterious disappearance of Mrs Quincey's hot cross buns at the town bakery. (Just for the record, they were later found in the warming drawer of the oven, much to her protest when she was accused of leaving them there.) The police were out of their depth; the people of Trincaster were in uproar and had even started locking their doors for the first time since 1936.

Ryan and Jake had to do something to help. This was a call to action for them, and Ryan knew there was a lot more to this than it seemed. Nothing ever happened in Trincaster, then all of a sudden an asteroid hits the town and a crime wave erupts. He believed this was the work of darker forces than just regular criminal activity. Maybe something landed with the asteroid; maybe there was something inside it; maybe it was a UFO, Ryan mused. Whatever it was had sent the residents crazy: people didn't even say hello in the streets any more.

The asteroid had been lifted out of their garden with a series of cranes and taken away, presumably for scientific testing, but no one really knew for sure. Some kids had spread rumours that it had been hijacked before it ever reached the test facility.

Ryan surveyed their house from the hill with his high-powered binoculars. Their garden and house were still completely out of bounds, covered with the kind of white tents you'd only see during a high-profile murder investigation. Hazard tape surrounded the property and armed guards were present around the clock. The only people allowed in or out of the area were scientists and police who donned white beekeeper-style suits with oxygen tanks strapped to their backs and arrived in strange unmarked white vans.

It would be nearly impossible to get inside there, but he knew that it held secrets that would help them unravel the mystery of what was going on. Ryan had to put the thought to the back of his mind, though, until he could work out how to break inside. For now, if they could focus on the crime wave, find some clues that the police had not noticed, then they could hopefully prevent anything else happening and discover what on earth was in that meteorite.

"Why don't we just distract that guy as he circles around the garages?" questioned Jake. "Surely that would be easier than breaking in and getting caught? I'm sure it would give us enough time to get close to the house." It was as though his brother had read his mind and followed his thought process. He kicked himself for not coming up with the idea first. He had to focus his mind. He mentally timed how long it took the man to finish a lap of the block: seven minutes and 53 seconds. If they set off now, they'd make it just in time.

"Let's go!" Ryan pulled his black ninja face mask and hood over his face: time for stealth. They set off down the hill at speed, weaving side to side, dodging and diving behind trees, plants and shrubs as they descended. Every minute or two they dropped to the ground to avoid the glare of the ever-circling search lights. Before long Ryan could see the back of the garage in clear view as he ducked down behind a low stone wall. The crisp early evening air filled his lungs as a knot began to form in his stomach. Maybe he'd underestimated the danger; maybe they weren't cut out for this.

"When I signal, you run that way and I'll make a dash for the house. If you can distract him for long enough, I should be able to get a good look in the garden and get some idea of what's going on. Do not reveal your identity under any circumstance!"

The guard rounded the corner, the crunch of his combat boots on the pebbly back alley unsettling them. He was so much bigger up close: a giant compared to the teenage boys.

"Remember what I've said. He's coming now," Ryan said in a hushed tone as the man neared their hiding place. Any second he would be right next to them.

"Look! On his neck, it's another one of those tattoos!" He could clearly see the same spiral formation he'd seen earlier on the policeman; maybe they were connected in some way.

"Now, go!"

Jake leapt up and over the wall, bolting off down the back alley.

"Come get me, you big bully!" he yelled, waving and taunting the guard as he ran.

The garish guard was taken completely unawares and momentarily paused in shock. As he regained his senses he lurched forward and his feet slid from underneath him. He nose-dived hard into the gravel with an almighty *crunch*, sending the contents of his pockets scattering across the alley. The man scrambled to his feet, quickly looking round to check no one had seen him fall and set off in pursuit of Jake.

As the guard disappeared into the distance Ryan popped his head up over the wall, immediately spotting a shiny artefact gleaming in the light over by the far side of the alley. He sprinted across and pocketed the object before rapidly spinning around to the left. He could hear voices: more guards were coming. He needed to get out of here, fast!

Chapter Seven

Dad had been acting really weirdly, which was unsurprising seeing as he'd lost his ex-wife, and his home had been all but destroyed in the accident. He was increasingly sharp with the twins; they knew there was no chance of compromise on anything. His mood swings had got worse and worse and the boys were at times scared to breathe too loudly for fear of reprimand.

Tea time was at 18:00 on the dot, consisting of a perfectly cooked plate of vegetables laid out in exactly measured portions on their plates. It looked like a diagram you'd see in a health book showing the ideal proportions of each food source to maintain the perfect physique. The boys were made to consume vast quantities of broccoli, cauliflower and sweet potato, which they hated more than anything on earth. Even when Jake vomited all over his plate, Dad just became even angrier.

"Eat it up now! This is what you get when the nation is fed genetically modified crap, creating a race of lazy and overweight people!" Dad snarled. "You can't even make it back on time for tea. I haven't the time to be hanging around waiting for you two!"

The boys knew better than to argue back; he was teetering on the edge and they didn't want to be the ones to push him over it. One false move would mean 100 press-ups, 100 sit-ups, 100 squat thrusts and 100 burpees, each of which was the last thing you needed after a mountain of steamed vegetables.

As soon as tea was finished and they'd eaten their three pieces of superfruit they were commanded to begin their two hours of homework and sent to their room. Dad thought they would have a lot of catching up to do after all the school they had missed, so was piling in extra work for them. Little did he know that Ryan would complete the work for both of them in less than three minutes, leaving the remainder of the time for superhero strategy planning.

It would be strange to be back at school after everything they had been through, but they were excited to get back to some semblance of normality. Dad made sure both boys were sitting at their desks, laptops ready, before he marched outside and locked himself in his man shed. Temporary though it was, Dad had come to regard the shed at this time as his own, and spent more time in it as he had in the one at their real home, before the asteroid hit.

Jake reckoned he was planning on producing the world's largest broccoli farm, thereby destroying the lives of millions and millions of poor veg-hating children. Ryan on the other hand, assumed he went into there to break down and cry out of sight of the boys. He had never been one to show any kind of emotion; he would rather die than show weakness.

As soon as they heard the clunk of the shed door, Ryan tipped out the contents of his pockets; his only concern was the shiny object he'd grabbed earlier.

On closer inspection, it was a silver metal tin, engraved with the same spiral pattern on the top as the policeman and guard had tattooed on them. It was the weight of a brick and sealed shut. Ryan noticed a miniature keyhole on the front.

"How are you going to open that? Do you reckon it's something valuable?"

Ryan didn't respond. Deep in concentration, he dragged over a cardboard box, filled with their few remaining possessions, scrambling through a plethora of pens, felt tips and sticky wrapper-less sweets before grabbing a little tub of paperclips. He still hadn't bothered to unpack the box and it had been weeks since he had moved in here.

"This should do the trick." In an instant he'd bent a small piece of metal into shape and as he was about to insert it into the lock, the little latch swung upwards. Ryan took a deep and sharp intake of air, and the lid of the tin raised itself as he thought about it as if through telekinesis.

Inside was a chunk of green glowing rock, weaved with tiny crystals, gleaming in the light. It was so beautiful, so pretty that Ryan couldn't take his eyes off it: he was transfixed. It was the most amazing thing he'd ever seen. He wondered how he could be so lucky to have something so incredible here in his hands. It was speaking to him, telling him what he must do. He had to obey.

"Stop it right now!" Jake leapt across and slammed the tin shut. "Control yourself!"

Ryan immediately came to his senses. What on earth was that? One second he had opened the tin with his mind and the next the contents had been taking it over. He needed to analyse this rock. If it could hypnotise him with his strong mind, then what could it do to others? How many people had been affected by this? How many had been marked with spiral tattoos? Who was in charge of all of this? There were too many questions and not enough answers. The situation was even darker and more disturbing than he'd first thought.

Chapter Eight

The ringing sound nearly made Jake jump out of his skin; he'd forgotten how loud the bell was after all that time off school. It was 13:00 and children flooded into the school building heading towards their next lesson, sighs ringing out along the corridor. It meant only one thing: IT class with Mr Bios. Jake heard Jimmy shouting down the corridor: "Jake, Ryan, come on, I'll race you!"

Jimmy was one of the only kids in school who could tell which twin was which and didn't have to go through the tedious rigmarole of working out who was who. Surely after all the years they had been at school the majority of these kids should be able to tell them apart by now.

Jimmy was a short, stubby lad with greasy, curly brown locks and massive, thick, black-rimmed glasses. He was their one true friend and always treated them as two individual people and not as the collective twins. He knew how much they hated being referred to as "the twins" and made a point of addressing them by their names in front of others. He was someone they could rely on completely, had never judged them and had always been there for them.

The three boys filed into the room, taking their usual position at the far side of the classroom. Mr Bios was sitting in his usual position hunched over his supercomputer, his eyes peeking over the top of the multiple screens he had in front of him. Bios was a curious man who clearly had more love for tech than real-life people. He was short, bald, had a sinister monobrow and bodily odour you could smell ten metres away. He always wore a short-sleeved off-white shirt with a dubious floral pattern, coupled with metal-framed glasses with a strange orange tint to them. Jake thought his voice sounded like bacon sizzling in a pan when he spoke.

"All open your laptops immediately. Today you will be working on your coding project again. I expect silence throughout the lesson. If anyone does require assistance, they should raise their hand to gain my attention."

He clearly had some geeky project that he was working on, probably the next waves of crime in Trincaster, thought Ryan. He would be the perfect candidate to be part of a weird crime gang. As though Bios was listening to his thoughts, Ryan felt his piercing, beady eyes focussing right on him over the top of his glasses, so he stooped his head to avoid eye contact. It was too late, though; he couldn't avert his gaze. He was transfixed by Bios' eyes, frozen in time: a statue glued to his seat. He became increasingly aware of the noises around him. *Tap, tap, tip, tap.* The sounds began to increase in volume until they became unbearable: *TAP, TAP, TAP, TAP* – everyone's fingers hitting the keys – *TAP, TAP, TAP, CLICK, TAP, KAA-BOOOOOM!!*

The school bell rang continuously; the noise was deafening. High-pitched squeals, screams, shouting and the stampede of teenage feet erupted everywhere. The toxic smell of burning plastic, wood and paper filled their nostrils as hot ash stuck to the outside windows and smoke bellowed into the room. There was chaos everywhere. Bios vanished completely; Ryan looked at the spot he'd been in in complete disbelief.

Jake leapt out of his seat, his laptop careering off into the air as he forged a pathway towards the fire-exit door; nothing was going to stand in his way. Ryan briskly followed in his footsteps at speed: it was like Moses parting the waves as students were swept aside.

The classroom door swung back so hard that it nearly smashed him in the face as he sprinted to catch his brother, heading straight towards the pandemonium.

Jake raced down the corridor, the screech of his rubber soles echoing against the white walls as he slid round corners, dodging and diving around disorientated students. He glimpsed a huge dark figure zooming down the corridor well ahead of them. Kids cowered against the walls. It couldn't be Bios, this man was far too big and fast.

He faced less and less pupils as he rounded another corner and was met with a fire door slamming shut. Jake immediately pushed through the metal door, skidding out into a deserted quadrant of the school yard around the back of the gym building. There wasn't a soul in sight, not a sound to be heard aside from the crash of the door as Ryan arrived looking like he'd run a marathon with a washing machine strapped to his back.

"We've lost them! Whoever that was is far too quick for us!" spat Jake as he slammed the flat of his hand into the exterior wall, caving in a few bricks in the process.

"Quick, look over there, climbing over the back wall."

Ryan pointed his arm across as the same bulky figure of a man, dressed head to toe in black, disappeared over the perimeter of the school.

"That's him! Quick, let's get after him," yelled Jake as he set off like an Olympic runner in hot pursuit of the hooded figure.

"JAKE! Get here now!"

He stopped in his tracks and turned to see the imposing figure of Mr Bridgestone standing at the fire exit with Jimmy standing sheepishly alongside him. They were busted! The boys' first chance at solving the crimes was a complete flop. Some superheroes they were, getting stopped by the Deputy Head before they were even close.

"We're trying to evacuate the building from a potential terrorist attack and you two head straight towards the danger. Come with me now!"

School was to be cancelled for the rest of the week while the tidy-up was completed and a temporary canteen was installed. A bomb had been planted in the school kitchen, blowing the slop they called Soup of the Day about two miles skywards. Fortunately, the dinner ladies had just finished for the day so no one was injured, but it was clear that ten minutes earlier and it wouldn't have been soup splattered everywhere.

When the boys eventually arrived back at their temporary home via a police escort, courtesy of Mr Bridgestone, they found Dad waiting for them.

"What are you doing here, Dad?" quizzed Jake.

"Work sent all the parents home due to the incident at school and I understand that you two clowns put yourselves in grave danger," replied Dad sternly. "So, if you think you're going to be lazing around for the rest of the week, then you'd better think again!"

At this, he marched over to the desk, opening a book entitled *Healthy Work Ethics* by Helen Shrowder.

"I want you both to read this book and be prepared for questioning later. You have two hours, starting now. Come on, what are you waiting for?"

He strode out of the room and headed straight for the shed.

Chapter Nine

Bang! The front door slammed shut and the boys were instantaneously wide awake; the alarm clock read 6:30am. Why on earth was Dad going out at this time in the morning? Probably some ridiculous marathon training or another fitness-based lunacy. Ryan jumped up and headed for the kitchen where he found *The Trincaster Gazette* strewn across the table and a half-drunk cup of black coffee still steaming on its coaster. There had been another crime in town and the boys hadn't even had the slightest inkling of any wrongdoings.

THE TRINCASTER GAZETTE

Massive Explosion at Chocolate Factory

Breaking news coming in this morning. Last night at around 11:30pm there was a huge explosion at Trincaster Chocolate Factory.

As the largest employer in the town, this is a complete disaster. Not only will this lead to massive unemployment, a spokesman estimates that the factory provides 50% of the food sources of the local economy.

Starvation is on the cards for the local people, many of whom have been spotted drinking chocolate from the factory waste pipe which leads into Trincaster Brook.

A policeman responded to the incident with a scratch of his head and a shrug of his shoulders.

"Come on, we need to get to base," said Ryan after showing Jake the newspaper. "Dad's out and we have some serious work to complete. This can't carry on any longer or there will be nothing left of this town."

Half an hour later and the boys were sitting in their lair, mulling over the evidence. The place had come along leaps and bounds since they initially constructed it. Metal sheeting lined the walls and bright lighting illuminated the space. A supercomputer to rival that of Mr Bios had been pieced together in a central segment of the room. Corridors off the main sector had been built, leading to further rooms, including an armoury, training facility/gym, garage and personal quarters. The place was by no means worthy of the great superheroes of the past but it was practical, functional and fulfilled every aspect they required from it.

Ryan was proud of how far they had come in such a short space of time.

"Have you seen what I've been developing?" He pulled out what looked like a skateboard without any wheels. "Look at this." He winked as he threw the board towards him and watched his brother's jaw drop in amazement as it hovered in mid-air in front of him. "Here's one for you too." He laughed as he chucked another one up alongside it. "And if you think that's cool, you ain't seen nothing yet."

He ushered Jake through into the armoury. "Open special weapons."

"Affirmative," a cybotic voice answered as the room transformed in front of them. Rows of cabinets filled with a whole variety of weapons that rose out of the floor: catapults, water pistols, nerf guns, paint grenades and more.

"And here is the grand finale: Reveal superpower suits!"

Jake's face lit up as the outfits lowered from the ceiling. A pair of yellow suits, complete with ST emblem, red capes and face masks.

"I've added some extra features which I'll show you later, but you have to admit that Grandma has done a great job. Why don't you try yours on?"

Jake didn't need a second invitation; he rapidly pulled down the suit and stretched it on. Ryan was soon in his too. Now he felt like they were the real deal, punching his arm in the air, putting on his cheesiest Hollywood impression. "Super Twin Power!" laughed Jake.

"I love it!" Ryan added. "Anyway, we're here to devise a strategy not suit up for battle."

The boys agreed that they needed a patrol around Trincaster as there was no way of determining what would happen next. There was no pattern they could

follow, and all the targets appeared to be completely random. If they could enlist the help of Jimmy, then unbeknown to him they could create a greater coverage of the area. This coupled with a web of micro-surveillance cameras that Ryan had developed would hopefully capture anything else going on and give them some vital clues to the mystery.

***

As they walked back home, they felt satisfied that they were closer to a breakthrough than before. Striding down the street, Ryan suddenly stopped dead in his tracks, pulling his brother down behind a battered car.

"Look over there, Jake. Aren't those three the police officers that escorted us home after we were in hospital?"

Jake was shocked to see that it was indeed the three men but not as they had seen them before. These guys looked extremely out of place, wearing clothes that reminded them more of punks than policemen. Handcuffs, truncheons and police badges had been replaced by leather studded jackets, tattoos and piercings.

"What do you reckon, Ryan? Are they undercover or what? That's hardly the image a squeaky-clean copper would like to portray, is it now!"

"Shhh, keep it down. I think quite the opposite is true. Maybe they aren't undercover policemen but rather they were undercover criminals when we saw them last time. We need to follow them and see what they're really up to. Hang on, look at the back of his jacket!" Painted in white was the large swirl pattern they kept seeing.

The three suspicious men bundled a large package into the back of a clapped-out old white van and moved around to the front. The skinny tall one looked all around him and pulled down his beanie hat over his eyes before flicking his burnt-out cigarette in the twin's direction. Ryan pulled Jake further down behind the car as the guys jumped into the van and skidded off.

"Go, go, go! We have to see where they are headed!"

Jake set off at breakneck speed down the adjacent back alley. If they could get down to the post office fast enough they would cut them off along the one-way street. The chase was on… Jake left a trail of dust in his wake. As he flew across the next junction, out of the corner of his eye he saw the van skidding around the corner. He zoomed across the road, narrowly missing a motorbike and charged onwards, the post office in his sight. He dodged left, then right past a handful of bewildered pedestrians, who saw nothing but a blur of limbs as he flew past them.

Approaching the building fast now, he expected the flash of the white van as it cut across in front of him any second now. He prepared for a hard right turn: fifty metres, twenty metres, ten metres. He slid across the Tarmac, leaning at 45 degrees, cornering like a speed skater, but where had it gone? The van had vanished!

"Where is it?" spluttered Ryan as he eventually caught up with his brother. "It's impossible, it's just disappeared!"

Jake looked completely bemused: their only lead had vanished into thin air. He ran up and down the street looking for any more clues but found nothing. They'd gone one step forwards and two back. Ryan, on the other hand, hadn't given up just yet. If these guys weren't who they said they were, maybe Dad was involved in this somehow. The spirals, the pieces of asteroid, the hypnotism: something clicked in his mind.

"We need to get home, now! We have to find out what is inside that shed..."

Chapter Ten

The padlock hit the concrete path with a giant thud. A creak worthy of a haunted mansion reverberated as the shed door rocked backwards and Ryan stepped inside.

"Well, this is the last thing I was expecting," said a startled Jake.

Rows and rows of potted plants and vegetables sat on neat wooden shelving units, all perfectly lined up at equidistant intervals, with lighting rigs shining upon each little block of seedlings. Ryan had expected some kind of high-tech armoury with robots organising an army of troops ready for war. He felt bad for suspecting his dad in the first place: it was nothing more than a potting shed. Their dad had been through a lot of trauma too, so of course he was going to be acting differently.

"I don't know why, but something is telling me this is all a set-up," reasoned Ryan, picking up a metal trowel and examining it from all angles.

"Hardly! Look out, we're in mortal danger: attack of the killer seedlings. Dad's lured us into his sinister shed where the pansies and roses rip us apart. We should never have suspected our own father."

"No, you twonk. This shed is a set-up! Think about it: do you just walk straight into our lair? No, it's disguised! This has to be a cover-up for what's really going on in here. There must be a secret entrance; I find it hard to believe Dad spends all his time in here potting plants."

"You're unhinged, Ryan. You think you have the answer to everything now!" he snarled as he turned his back on his brother.

Ignoring his twin, Ryan set to work searching the shed, picking up plants and carefully putting them back, combing the floor for a trapdoor. Smoothing his hands along the grainy wall panels, he searched for a hidden lever or button, to no avail.

"This is pointless. Let's just get that padlock back on the door and get out of here. Dad will kill us if he comes back and finds us snooping."

Ryan could see that Jake was getting increasingly frustrated with the situation and had convinced himself that he was losing his mind as he scoured every nook and cranny of the shed, painstakingly. Ryan analysed every little knot in the wood and raised bump. He had to find something: he couldn't be so far wrong.

"That's it!" snapped Jake. "I've had enough of this. You can get busted by Dad on your own, but I've had as much as I can take." He spun on his heel, back out onto the stone path, kicking a large boulder at the side.

Clunk, whiz, ting! He whirled around immediately to see Ryan's whole body lowering downwards at speed along with the inside structure of the shed. In an instant his head disappeared from view and Ryan was no more. The inside of the shed slid back up and clicked into place. Jake must have triggered an entrance switch. He had to go after his brother – he could be in grave danger. He kicked the rock again hard, dived into the shed, pulling the door shut behind him. Nothing happened...

Then all of a sudden, the place sprang into life. The inner skeleton of the shed transported him downwards under the ground as all light disappeared around him. He was a miner heading down the pits, putting his whole life in jeopardy; he was just lacking a candle and a canary. He could feel his heart beating out of his chest, his legs shaking as his eyes began to grow accustomed to the darkness.

The lift ground to a halt, the wall opened up in front of him and he squinted at the bright LED lights running along the ceiling of the hollowed-out passageway in front of him. Ryan must be along here somewhere, he thought as he began to creep down the corridor.

CRUNCH! He nearly jumped out of his skin as he swivelled around to see the wall close up behind him. Only one way to go now, he thought to himself as he continued on his tiptoes. At the end of the tunnel he was met by a solid stone doorway. He firmly pushed the door open and could not believe his eyes.

A huge cavern brightly lit with stadium-sized floodlights faced him, clinical and white. One wall was flanked with a large board of what looked like computers; there were buttons and dials everywhere, and a large shiny metal table sat in the middle of the room. On it were a carefully arranged collage of news clippings, articles and books. On the back wall was a jumbo-sized map of Trincaster, pins stabbed in at various points. Bright red string joined the points, forming an intricate spider's web across the wall.

On the left-hand wall there were various metal cupboards of assorted sizes and on the far-left corner was a steel doorway that had been left open. Jake crept across the room, feeling like even the sound of his breathing was too loud. As he got closer to the doorway, his ears pricked up at a faint scuttling sound. Maybe it's rats, he thought to himself. Or even worse, aliens that have come to earth inside that meteorite!

Anything was possible after the last few weeks. Everything he had known to be real and normal, had been blown into smithereens. Now here he was in some strange underground bunker, his heart in his mouth, creeping towards a door that could lead to anywhere.

"Boo!"

Ryan leapt from the doorway, arms held up like a vicious raptor, a huge cheeky grin on his face.

"You're a doughnut, you scared the living daylights out of me!" snapped Jake.

"Well, who else did you think it would be? You knew I was the only one down here," laughed Ryan.

"How did I know that? Anything could have happened to you, down here by yourself!"

"Your face, though. I wish I could have taken a picture. You looked like you'd seen a ghost. What do you think of this place, then? It puts our place to shame, doesn't it?"

"Yeah, it sure does. It looks like Dad has been busy. I can't believe that we have an evil dad; I feel sick even saying the words."

"Look over here." Ryan pointed across at the map. "Have you seen all this?"

The boys wandered over and began to study it: all the places that had been attacked or targeted by crime were marked by black pinheads. There were, however, a multitude of other locations marked with red pins, which the boys could only assume were the next round of targets, disturbingly.

It seemed their Evil Dad was targeting all their favourite places: the cinema, bowling alley and every fast-food takeaway in town. Did he really hate them that much that he was hell-bent on destroying everything that they knew and loved? He had completely lost it, that much was for sure. The meteorite had changed him beyond recognition. He may have been strict before but he was still their dad; he still loved and cared for them. Goodness knows what he was capable of now – this underground hideout had proved that. Was he even classed as their dad any more or their arch-nemesis?

The boys stopped and looked at each other and felt an intimate connection that went further than any twin connection they had ever experienced before. They didn't just know what each other was thinking: they were speaking to each other through their minds.

"We have to do it, don't we?!" uttered Jake.

"Yes," said Ryan firmly. They both knew what had to be done. Dad or no Dad, they had to stop this criminal and bring him to justice, right now. Jake nodded in approval and punched his right fist into his left with a resounding thud. As his hands connected with a snap, the lights went off and the room was plunged into complete darkness. There was that scuffling noise again as the boys were grabbed from behind, hit over the head and dragged off along the cold, hard floor.

Chapter Eleven

The straps started to dig into Jake's wrists and even though he knew that one squeeze of his arms would break the binding, he had to see what and who he was up against. For all he knew he could find a sawn-off shot gun pointed against his head at any minute.

His head throbbed with pain but at least he had plenty of brain cells to spare, despite what his brother thought. Dots of light penetrated the microscopic holes in the hood covering his head; the smell of dried blood filled his nostrils, and he heard the sound of metal crunching against metal. He would only need a second to escape, but at the same time he couldn't let on to Dad that he had super strength. This was definitely something he needed to make use of just at the right time. Besides, Ryan was the brains: he was relying on him to concoct a genius master plan to get them out of this sticky situation.

Suddenly, two hands whipped the hood from his head. He immediately screwed his eyes tightly shut as the light was blinding. He was sitting on a chair in the centre of a bright white room, the size of which he couldn't comprehend. His brother sat facing him, a terrified look across his face, bound to a chair with leather straps around his ankles and wrists.

Standing directly to the side of the Super Twins was a large, domineering figure, cloaked in black. The only distinguishable human features they could make out was a pair of piercing eyes staring right through them.

"What made you think you could trespass on my property and live to tell the tale? You have no right to be here; you will suffer the consequences!" He spoke in an incredibly low, gravelly tone, with purpose and intent.

"What did you expect to find? Have you even the slightest idea of the beautiful project we are working on here?"

The boys sat there dumbstruck for a second before Jake drew the courage to answer back.

"You're the evil person, who is destroying our town and we are going to stop you! We … we thought you were our dad but we were stupid to think that. He would never have been a part of this and committed the evil crimes that you have!"

The hooded man intently glared at the boy.

"Evil? You are mistaken. My actions are merely a response to the evil acts which plague this town on a daily basis. I am building an army to combat the hideous and corrupt nature of Trincaster and you, my boy, are trying to spoil the performance." At this, the man pulled

back his hood to reveal his true identity. His jaw was clenched, a grimace monopolising his face, eyebrows sunk deep over his eyes, a blank stare going right through them. There was no emotion other than hatred.

Here standing in front of them was not their dad but an Evil Dad, practically unrecognisable from the man they knew. Whoever or whatever he was now, one thing was for sure: they were in mortal danger. He didn't seem to know who the boys were, and if he did, they meant nothing to him any more.

"I am doing this for you. I'm doing this for all of us – it's in everybody's best interests. Do you think for one second these were just random attacks? Can't you see the huge difference this will make to us all? Healthy bodies make healthy minds!"

The boys were now convinced he'd totally lost the plot.

"Healthy bodies and healthy minds?!" exclaimed Jake. "You think by bombing everywhere and destroying half the town that will make people's lives better? You must be joking! What has happened to you? One day you're our father and the next, half of our town has been obliterated and you are the one responsible!" Ryan was exasperated: his words didn't seem to be having any impact on Evil Dad.

"We have to destroy him. It's not our dad anymore: his mind has been taken over. The asteroid has made him into something else!" Ryan spoke through their mind connection. His hands began to shake as the realisation dawned on him that this could mean the end of their real dad too. Jake could feel the emotion emanating through his brother.

"Agreed — we don't have a choice. We either take our chances or we die in the process. If I rip out of these restraints, can you distract him enough for me to gain an advantage?"

It was too late, though. The evil version of Dad stared deep into Ryan's eyes. He could feel his father's thoughts trying to push into areas of his mind he was not welcome. Trying to alter his beliefs and everything he considered just and right. Sweat began to pour off Ryan's brow: it was taking every ounce of his mental strength to push back the vile brainwaves.

Jake burst through his shackles, powering towards the crazed imposter. "Noooooo!" he yelled as he closed in on the villain. Dad swung round towards him, breaking the mental connection with his brother and shooting electric lightning bolts from his fingertips. Jake flew high across the room, landing in a heap on the floor, his clothes smouldering.

Ryan, seizing his opportunity, focussed his mind fiercely and entirely on their enemy. Feeling the energy flow through his body, he lifted Dad off his feet and into the air, swinging him and rotating him in a mid-air cartwheel. Ryan felt a surge of fire through his body, gaining a greater control of the power. He tightened his grip on the man, squeezing his neck with his mind. Dad clutched his neck with his hands, struggling to breathe, choking as it condensed.

Out of desperation, Dad hit a button on his arm. Sirens sounded and all around them doors opened. As heavily armed henchmen appeared from every angle, Dad dropped out of the air. There were too many men: the boys were trapped.

Chapter Twelve

How many days they had been there God only knows. Ryan and Jake were woozy and weak. Dad must have drugged them or drained them with mind-power techniques. Either way, they could hardly move, had no concept of time whatsoever or even where they were. As Ryan came back into the land of consciousness, he quickly established that they were still underground from the air vents high up in the wall. They were lying on thin mattresses, a small table in between them with a tray of food (veg) and two glasses of water neatly placed beside them. At the opposite end of the room stood a solid metal door with a hatch in it. It was a prison cell. How on earth would they get out of this?

Jake sat there staring into space. This was it: they were trapped in this forsaken cell for the foreseeable future unless something miraculous happened. How could their lives have come to this?

"What the heck are we going to do now? We need to get out of here: I can't cope!" At this, Jake slammed his hands into the cold, solid wall, barely making a dint in it. This wasn't any ordinary cell: it was reinforced with the strongest material he'd ever encountered.

Ryan stared across at his brother thoughtfully; as usual he was five steps ahead. In his super brain he had already escaped, found Evil Dad, captured him, destroyed his followers and converted him back to regular but slightly annoying normal Dad.

"There is potentially a way of getting us out of here, but it will require our combined skills and an element of luck."

Jake wasn't on the same wavelength at all. All he could think of was inhaling the ridiculously plain and boring food before smashing his way through the six-foot, thick, solid prison door.

"I can see what you're considering, Jake, and it's impossible, even with your super strength. I estimate you're at no more than 47 per cent of your regular strength, and that door is designed to hold off an entire army. Our only hope is to try and escape through the air conditioning system."

Jake's ears began to prick up as he looked up to the vent, which must have been ten feet up on the wall.

"If you put your all into it, I'm sure you could throw me up there. It might take a couple of attempts to get the cover off but I'm sure it's possible. Once I crawl through, I'm sure I can find a way of opening this cell from the outside and letting you out."

Ryan continued to rattle through his orders whilst Jake's sole concern was finishing the plate of veg. He was so hungry even this actually tasted OK. He let an almighty gust of wind out of his backside as he polished off the last of the Brussel sprouts.

"Is there any need for that? It absolutely stinks: I can barely breathe in here as it is!" Ryan wafted the air with his hands, but it was a pointless exercise. "Surely you've had enough food now? Come on ... give me a leg up."

Ryan climbed up via the wall onto Jake's outstretched hands and was launched high up into the air. He clawed at the grate but missed it completely, coming crashing down to the ground and yelling out in pain.

"Again?" quizzed Jake.

"Give me a minute, you twit. You could have caught me, instead of watching me miss the grille and injure myself."

"Well, why don't you use your telekinetic power to loosen the cover from down here? At least then you'll have a ledge to grab onto."

Ryan stared up at the air vent, concentrating his efforts on the screws. One by one they started to pop out and drop to the floor, with the grate hitting the solid concrete last. The stench of Jake's fart lingered in the air. Ryan attempted to breathe through his mouth instead.

"That will do the trick. Right, throw me up again but this time higher, and if I miss, you need to catch me, all right?"

Jake did as he was asked and watched as Ryan's feet soon disappeared inside the hole. Jake was on his own now.

He sat on the floor, hoping to goodness that his brother wouldn't get caught. He was on edge as he watched a spider crawling up the wall next to him, completely unaware that it was as trapped as he was. Seconds passed by like minutes, minutes like hours. Maybe Ryan had been caught and was being tortured by ruthless gang members. Maybe they were on their way to come to take him and torture him too.

A big booming noise echoed from the solid door as it slowly began to move outwards, and in walked Jimmy, closely followed by Ryan.

"What on earth are you doing here? How did you know we were here?" Jake jumped up in delight.

"You guys have been missing for days! A lot has changed since I last saw you. Half of the town is now part of this evil zombie army; the crimes have been obscene. I joined the freedom fighters to save our town and have been chosen for reconnaissance missions due to my compact size. I have had this place under surveillance: I had an inkling you would be in here. I managed to sneak in through the air conditioning system and had the shock of my life when I came face to face with Ryan."

"But how did you know we'd been captured?"

"I know you guys better than anyone so it wasn't hard for me to work out what was happening. The way you kicked into action during the school bombing: it was clear you had changed from the ordinary twins that you were. No kid would run straight towards danger to save the school and catch the culprits. Most would celebrate the place being blown up!" Jimmy laughed at his own quick wit. "If you had powers of any sort then you were the biggest threat to the evil army and you had to have been captured. The way they get inside people's minds made you two potentially a very powerful weapon." Jimmy smiled as he spoke, secretly pleased that his two best friends were potential superheroes.

"We need to get out of here, fast! There are guards patrolling everywhere so we need to be cautious. Keep close to me and follow my every instruction. I have a blueprint of this place on my navigation watch so I'll take us on the quickest route out of here!"

The boys slipped and sneaked down corridors, avoiding the armed guards. Jimmy stealthily led the way down passageways and through arches until he halted Ryan and Jake in their tracks.

"This way, we're nearly out now." They turned the corner, slipped through a door and they were hit with bright sunlight. They had made it.

When their eyes had adjusted, what they saw threw them into complete shell shock. From where they stood on the side of Cragbert Hill, they could see the town centre had descended into complete anarchy. A huge angry mob was rioting down the main street, and grey smoke filled the air – the result of burning buildings. Car alarms wailed, sirens sounded, people were shouting and screaming.

The Super Twins had to do something, and quickly! Jimmy chucked a pair of binoculars at Ryan; through them he could see the town had been split in two. On one side of the high street the rioters and looters, led by Evil Daddy, were creating absolute carnage, destroying everything in their path. Lines and lines of zombie-like army members carried out their orders, marching in a hypnotic rhythm with each other, armed and dangerous. They were hell-bent on causing chaos and destruction: nothing would stand in their way.

In the middle of the main street, the remaining factions of the town had made a huge ten-foot-high barrier made of anything they could find. It contained traffic cones, signs, shopping trolleys, rubbish bags and even a rusty old bike had been thrown on top. It was holding back the brain-washed masses for now but it wouldn't keep them at bay forever. People were hiding down back alleys, barricading themselves inside, scared to come out of their homes. Curtain twitchers were in their element, excitedly watching the crazy events unfold.

Jimmy said the people were scared, lacking strong leadership, completely disorganised. Aside from the huge wall, they had done little or nothing to confront the angry army. The police were a mile out of town, scared to even enter Trincaster, hiding in their police cars, watching from a safe distance, only concerned with their own safety.

"We have to do something, now!" declared Jake. "We need to get to the base, collect our weapons, galvanise these people and launch a full-scale attack! We don't know what they are capable of. If we don't hurry, the whole town will be destroyed!" He was getting agitated as he spoke; he couldn't watch any more.

"You two head back to your base and make the necessary preparations. I need to return to Headquarters, speak to the alliance leader and arrange a meeting with you." He chucked a video watch at Ryan. "Keep hold of this communication device. All you have to do is touch this button on the side and you'll be able to contact me immediately. Good luck."

The Super Twins leapt into action, heading straight for their base. Over the hilltop they ran, determination etched across their faces. All their preparation had been leading up to this moment: this was what they had been waiting for. Evil Dad wasn't going to get the better of them this time – that was for sure, thought Ryan. Not when they were fully armed, dangerous and with an army of followers behind them ready to save their town.

As Ryan arrived at their base, stopping to allow the iris scanner to check his identity before admission, he felt an overwhelming sense of achievement in what they'd accomplished. He looked across at his brother as they entered the base.

"Mum would be proud, you know." He could see the comment really touched his brother.

"I wish she was here to see how far we've come. I

know she had her flaws, but she'd be our biggest cheerleader right now, I'm sure of it," replied Jake as a tear rolled down his cheek.

"We not only have to do it for her, we have to do this for everyone else, not just this town but the next one. We must be victorious; we have to be the heroes that Trincaster has been waiting for.

Ryan gave his brother a massive high-five, but at the moment of impact felt something he'd never felt before. An incredible surge of energy spread from his body through to his brother's and back, an unstoppable twin connection.

"Can you feel that?"

It was as though his powers had been magnified tenfold: he had inherited his brother's strength as well as his own hyper-intelligence. They had combined into one superhuman. He felt shockwaves tingling at his fingertips. He was supercharged; they were supercharged! Jake pulled away, reeling in shock.

"Whooaa! That ... that felt incredible. What on earth just happened?"

"I think we just discovered our final superpower. Did you feel that energy at your fingertips? We truly are ready, ready to release a supersonic seismic shockwave!"

Ryan headed through into the armoury, suiting up and preparing the weapons. He grabbed every gizmo and gadget they had, strapping water blasters, paint guns and all manner of battle kit to himself and Jake.

They certainly looked the part in their identical, bright yellow and red outfits. Nobody was going to miss them, that was for sure.

Bleep, bleep! Ryan jumped as the communication device sounded on his wrist: Jimmy was on video call.

"Hey guys, I've set up a meeting with Vortex the rebel leader. He's keen to meet you and gain your trust.

You need to make it down to the old council offices pronto and be stealthy. Evil Dad has his spies out and we don't need to attract any unwanted attention."

Chapter Thirteen

"I thought you were told to be inconspicuous?" Vortex looked the Super Twins up and down; he was disgusted with what he saw. "You two are hardly the heroes I was expecting to see, but I may yet be proven wrong." At present all he could see in front of him were two kids dressed in bright yellow suits, about as discreet as a baby giraffe hiding in a herd of goats.

Had it really got so desperate as to pin the hopes of the nation on two inexperienced teenage boys? Maybe he was getting too old for this game after all. He stroked his long white beard as the Super Twins walked further into the boardroom, heading towards the remaining two chairs at the large, oval table.

"Please be seated. We need to be swift in our business; we don't have much time. I understand you've been briefed by Gold Shield on the current situation." Vortex motioned to Jimmy as he spoke, who raised an eyebrow in acknowledgement. "Evil Dad has gained a considerable amount of ground in the last few days: we are on the back foot and pinned against a brick wall. Reinforcements are non-existent. I don't know how much longer we can dig in. We've been closely looking at an exit strategy as all may already have been lost. It may be the best option to cut our losses and escape while we can."

The boys jumped to their feet, sending their chairs reeling back behind them.

"You bring us down here to your shiny little office to insult us and tell us you're planning on running away from any conflict?" Vortex could see the anger flowing out of Ryan as he yelled across the French polished table at him. "We came here to make a difference, to fight back and defeat this evil army, not to listen to the negative rants of a washed-out old man!"

Vortex was taken aback by this: maybe they were the real deal after all.

"We need all your best intel," continued Ryan. "I want locations, number of troops, weapons we're facing and any other details you know. We are here to lead this army not to run away and hide."

This meeting has just done a 180-degree spin, thought Vortex. He stood and walked over to the large screen behind him as he began to click away at the pointer in his hand.

"Here are the positions of the evil forces right now: here, here and here. Their army outnumbers us two to one and has far more advanced weaponry that we have. They do have their weaknesses, though. From what we can gather they are controlled from a central point through this panel in the centre of their chest plates. If we can hit this then it tends to disable the fighters. They may as well be robots: each section tends to behave in a similar fashion when the swirl glows green." He pointed to all the different areas but as he spoke the image cut out completely, before a crackling, fuzzy image formed in front of his eyes.

"Sorry to interrupt your little presentation there, Vortex. I have to say you were doing a marvellous job." Evil Dad smiled the evillest of smiles as he spoke. "I can see you've got the Super Twins alongside you now, so maybe now you won't be such a scaredy-cat and run away like you were planning. If you decide to man up and face a real fight, be on Wheatsheaf Field at noon tomorrow. The battle lines have been drawn!"

The image cut to a black screen. Members of the alliance jumped up from the table and ripped the cables and connections out.

"I think it's too late for that now, Mr Vortex, sir," said Jake sarcastically. "Time for the Super Twins to take control and prepare for battle. All those in favour, raise their hands."

Chapter Fourteen

Whoosh, booom, crash, crack!

The tree split in two, just to the side of Jake, careering down and missing Kal from the kebab house by a pitta bread's width. This was it: the battle had begun.

Evil Dad stood bolt upright in the centre of his forces, black hood covering his head, a solid wooden staff, topped with a chunk of green meteorite, raised high in the air. Eyebrows furrowed, staring straight across the battlefield, he was ready to destroy the Super Twins. His army was organised into battalions – blocks of 100 soldiers, reminiscent of Roman legions, alert and awaiting his every gesture and command. He spun the staff in an exaggerated motion, sweeping it around and to the right.

"Attack!" came the blood-curdling scream.

His troops began to march forwards, their feet stamping in perfectly synchronised unison, their eyes fixated in front of them.

Stamp, stamp, stamp!

Jake and Ryan stared in awe. This was no civilian army: they were an army of vicious, highly trained, bloodthirsty zombies. Seeing the army advancing towards them gave them a spine-tingling chill. This had become very real, very quickly.

To their left, Gold Shield headed a platoon of eager resistance fighters: young, quick, able and ready to prove their worth. To the right, Vortex led a band of seasoned warriors: rough, rugged and battle-scarred; these were seasoned professionals, ready to roar into battle and show the others how it was done. The Super

Twins stood in the centre in front of the remaining forces: willing civilians, little or no experience of fighting but prepared to give their lives for their beloved homeland.

"Fire!!" Evil Dad's orders echoed across the field as his troops crouched into formation, solid blocks of soldiers providing protection as those behind launched missiles over the top, toppling several of the boys' team to the ground.

"Defensive block!" Jake screamed at the top of his voice. At his command his forces of willing (if not slightly petrified) fighters raised bin lids and baking trays over their heads to produce the most makeshift protective layer modern warfare had ever seen. Solid metal missiles and the occasional handmade smoke bomb clattered off their shields as the Twins' army stood resilient.

This was not as the Super Twins had planned. Evil Dad was in control and had an early advantage, while the boys hadn't launched an offensive move yet and their fighters were dropping like injured flies.

"Tighten up the ranks!" bawled Ryan at the cobbled-together army. "Keep those shields high and your guards up!"

The troops did as they were instructed, but they had to launch their attack immediately. They had to gain the upper hand, or they would all be wiped out before they had even got started.

The plan was simple. Vortex and Gold Shield were to advance their troops forward, engaging the legions of evil army while Jake was to lead a section of their best armed men back and around the side of the field, through the woods and attack the evil army from the right, catching them unawares. He was to attack hard with speed, taking out the right flank before Ryan drove

his troops forward, converging in the middle, for the final battle between Evil Dad and the Super Twins at close quarters.

Vortex took the lead, charging forwards and straight into the first legion, spinning wildly as he bashed into the opposition's shields with his two great hammers, sending the zombie troops wheeling backwards through the air. He appeared as a blur of blue and white from above as he ploughed into the thick of the action, in stark contrast to the black uniform of the enemy army.

Not one to be outdone by the old man, Gold Shield advanced his men too, determined to prove himself to his superhero friends. They clattered into another squadron, pushing their way through with their shields into the centre, before releasing miniature timed paint bombs and retreating. The resulting explosions sent the now multicoloured opposition running in opposite directions. Goldshield stopped his troops out on the left of the field, awaiting further orders.

Vortex radioed through on the intercom: "We have the enemy on the back foot…" It immediately cut out: he'd been hacked again.

Jake didn't need a second hint and immediately set off, scooting down behind the hedgerow and into the woods, leading his team of willing men at a swift pace, through the dense undergrowth, stopping every few hundred metres so the men could keep up and catch their breath. If they weren't quick, they would rapidly lose the element of surprise. Evil Dad would soon catch on and counter their attack; the zombified army would regroup in a flash. Something was telling him Dad had a lot more up his sleeve.

He was soon in position. Jake had crawled through the undergrowth until he could see the whole battlefield in front of them; they were perfectly placed. The soldiers crawled up behind, taking their positions, ready for the order to charge, weapons pointed on their targets. It was now down to the twins' mind connection to instigate the attack.

"Secondary forces, attack!" Evil Dad's blood-curdling scream was still echoing as engines roared into life. Motorbikes accelerated and emerged through the centre of the evil forces, a devastating wall of machines and black helmets heading straight for Ryan's heroes.

"Hold the line!" yelled Ryan as the bikes approached.

"Hold it, wait for it … now!"

Washing poles, long wooden spears and sticks were all raised up like lances and jabbed towards the wall of machines. The chaos Ryan's troops inflicted was immense. The brutal dark battalion fractured at its seams as riders flew through the air and motorbikes skidded off out of control. Bikes and injured zombie bodies were strewn across the field; Ryan's nostrils were filled with the stench of petrol and blood.

They had to regroup and quickly before the evil army sent in another shockwave.

"Ryan, Ryan it's Vortex…" A battered and bruised fighter limped his way up to the Super Twin as two more wounded soldiers carried the limp body of Vortex up to him. "He's out cold!" he cried out.

"Enough is enough!" roared Ryan. "We need to finish this once and for all." The men crowded around him as he rose in volume. "For many of you Vortex has been a leader, a friend, someone to look up to. We will not put up with this any longer. We will stand firm, we will stand strong, we will fight back!"

He slowly began to move forward, his head held high, raising his hands in the air.

"Charge!!" The command echoed over the battlefield and ricocheted within Jake's mind.

Over from the bushes the Super Twin led the attack, roaring as they steamrolled towards the enemy, his troops firing water blasters and rubber bullets covering him. The dark army started to fall and screams rang out over the grassy war zone. Jake powered into a mass of soldiers, sending bodies reeling backwards. Missiles rained down upon the remaining zombie warriors, tins of beans, spaghetti hoops and petit pois. The legion began to retreat, in complete disarray.

"They're on the run, keep on the offensive!" yelled Jake.

Ryan watched the attack in slow motion. Evil Dad's army had contorted at one side, no longer a perfectly formed battalion. Ryan sensed the opportunity and pushed his forces forwards through the centre of the battlefield, a solid rectangle of metal bin lids and handmade shields advancing upon the enemy. They had outmanoeuvred Evil Dad; the plan was working.

As Evil Dad's army was sent into confusion his jaw clenched as his eyes quickly surveyed the damage to his forces on the far left.

"Return to your positions now!" Dad's tone raised as he screamed his orders. The earth vibrated as troops regrouped into their huge blocks, eyes not deviating from the battle ahead.

Jake and Ryan had caused some serious damage to the black heart of the opposition. The boys' minds connected: *"Now is the time!"*

They looked across the field at each other; they had to head straight for Dad.

"Attack!" they both screamed in perfect synchronicity, willing their troops forwards. They blasted, smashed and slugged their way through the battlefield, determined to deliver the killer blow to the evil leader. *Boom!* Ryan sidestepped as a bomb landed and a crater appeared next to him. That was close!

The boys converged in the middle of the field, face to face with their arch-nemesis, the man who was once their father. It was time for a fight to the death…

Chapter Fifteen

This was it: the moment they had been waiting for. They stood staring down at Evil Dad, injured bodies of the local townspeople strewn around them. Ryan wondered how it had all come down to this. What was it even about in the first place? He thought back to times of happiness with his dad, laughing, joking, smiling, and now here he was ready to destroy him. Was this even the same man who stood before him? They had already lost their mother; how would they cope losing their father too?

"I don't know if I can do this," said Jake through their mind connection. "He's the only one who has ever been there for us. We can't kill our own father – think of all the good times we've had. This won't just destroy him; it will destroy me too!"

"It's too late to reminisce about the past. You have to remember this is not our dad – it's another version of him. The meteorite has taken over his brain!"

Jake looked across at his twin and nodded; they knew what had to be done. Ryan lifted rocks and pieces of rubble from the ground with his mind, firing them at Evil Dad, who just battered them away with his staff as if they were annoying little mosquitoes. His brother made a lunge for the supervillain and his super pace got him within centimetres of the man before he too was battered back.

Ryan had to focus, to break him down from the inside. He summoned all his power, pushing inside Evil Dad's mind, trying to find a weakness to gain any sort of advantage possible. He could feel the full force of the blackness inside there, pushing back against him, shielding Dad's dark and unyielding thoughts.

"Resistance is futile. You cannot infiltrate my mind: I am too powerful for you. You will join my cause, give in to the darkness, become one of us!" The voice was unbearable, shaking his skull from the inside.

"I will never succumb to you, never! As long as I live, I will fight till my dying breath!"

He could feel the anger and rage as Evil Dad sucked all his energy away. *Smash!* Dad drove the butt of his staff down hard into the dirt. The ground cracked open and the earth trembled. Bolts of electrical energy burst from the eye of his evil crook, encapsulating them, electrocuting them, rendering them defenceless, helpless.

Ryan rolled over, desperate to reach his twin, crawling, dragging his body towards him, closer and closer. He was dying, holding out his hand, stretching as far as he could as Jake did the same. Their hands connected with a snap, and the power of the Super Twins was realised. The super seismic shockwave emanated from them immediately and sent Evil Dad soaring into the air and smashing down to earth with a thud. Ryan and Jake slowly rose to their feet; they had him exactly where they wanted him.

Jake looked at his twin, grabbed his dad and lifted him high into the air by his shoulders. He had to destroy him: enough was enough. Thoughts flashed through his mind. When they had been given superpowers, what had gone so wrong as to turn their dad into an evil villain?

"Dad, why?" shouted Ryan, cutting the silence in two.

His father stared blankly back at him. It was as though nothing had registered in his brain; he just hung in the air, limp and defeated.

"Dad it's me, Ryan! Why are you doing this? Do you even know who I am?" There was a tremble in his voice; he couldn't hold back his emotions.

"You are the only obstacle that is holding me back from producing a perfect world," their dad finally retaliated, the monologue soon coming thick and fast. "The two people stopping me from making this town into what it always should have been – a symbol of Britain. Strong, organised, healthy and powerful. Free from bad foods, media influence and fun. This great nation was built on hard work and hearty, healthy, home-cooked vegetables. I am showing an example to the country of how things should be – an example to the world!"

The words began to rasp from his lips with a rat-a-tat-tat machine gun precision.

"You still have a choice to stand with me. Together we can make this place great; we can rule this country and make it great again!"

For the first time since the asteroid, he looked down and saw the face of his son staring back at him.

Jake lowered the man down to the ground. He couldn't do it; he couldn't kill him. Despite the heinous crimes he had committed, this was still his dad. The man who had made him, the man who had always been there for him, the man who took him in when his mother had died. He hooked his fist hard into the man's jaw. *Crack!* Evil Dad dropped to the floor in a heap. Jake jumped on top of his back, pushing his knee into his spine. It was over; the only place for him now was jail.

The engine grumbled as the army vehicle rolled up to them over the muddy field. Two soldiers jumped out and grabbed Evil Dad, before cuffing him and chucking him in the back of the armoured truck.

A large officer approached the boys. "I don't know how you managed it, but you've saved the town. You're heroes!"

Jake looked at Ryan; Ryan looked at Jake. "This is just the beginning," they simultaneously said in their minds. "We aren't heroes – we're superheroes," added Jake for everyone to hear.

Chapter Sixteen

The vehicle swerved and skidded across the rough terrain as the soldier avoided the injured bodies littering the ground. Just through this big muddy patch, and they would be back on the nice smooth road. This had been the craziest day he'd had since he enlisted. The tension had been rising for a while, but he never in his wildest imagination expected to see a battle on this scale.

He'd wanted to be in the thick of the action but had been forced to wait in the camouflaged Land Rover on standby. Apparently, orders had come from high up, completely out of his pay grade. He was assured that he could play a vital role, but he didn't know how that would be the case sitting in a truck a mile away waiting for orders to move in. Maybe now he would be rewarded. After all, he was the one bringing Evil Dad back to the compound.

"Will you shut your mouth while you eat; you look like a sheep chewing!"

His partner looked across at him with that idiotic expression he had come to loathe. Bits of banana were stuck in his beard and had fallen into his helmet on his knee. How on earth had he got partnered up with this imbecile? He knew he was better than this; he knew he was destined for greatness. During training he was streets ahead of the others, physically fitter, mentally stronger and more astute. The Sergeant had fast-tracked him through stages of the training and he'd scored top marks in the written exams.

"What's your problem?" mumbled Galbraith in his broad Scottish twang, his mouth still half full of banana.

"You're my problem, you moron. Just shut your mouth and stop talking when you eat. You only had to wait fifteen minutes and we'd be back at the prison block."

The look on his face told Galbraith it wasn't worth reacting to the comment. He was prone to moments of extreme violence when he lost his cool. Most of the others on his corps had learned to keep well out of his way when he was ready to snap, and this was definitely one of those times.

Thud, thud, thud! He felt the reverberations through the van as he rounded a corner at speed. It sounded as if their prisoner was now rolling around in the back. Not to worry, their destination was just down this road, and if they wanted a chauffeur service then they could find some other chump to drive the meat wagon.

He pulled up at the gate, greeted by a host of guards armed with SA80 rifles pointed at them.

"Show your ID documentation," the head guard drawled. "What is your purpose?"

"We have the prisoner. Open up now – generals' orders."

The guard waved across to another soldier who raised the barrier and ushered them through. He drove through, giving the men a death stare, and looped the Land Rover Defender round the back of the prison block. Another group of officers in bomb suits surrounded the vehicle whilst they used bomb detectors to check for unwanted devices. They jumped out and stood with their arms raised in the air whilst they were scanned too, before they moved round to the back of the van.

Galbraith opened the back door and out stepped Evil Dad.

"Good work, Gedeon. Take off these cuffs; we have much to do. The Super Twins should have finished me while they had the chance…"

THE END

Have you enjoyed reading *The Super Twins*?
Well then, please, please leave me a review on Amazon
or scan this QR code to take you straight there:

Without these reviews I wouldn't be able to pursue my
hopes and dreams of becoming a full-time author and
you definitely won't be reading *The Super Twins* sequel.
Obviously, I want you to be honest with your feedback;
nobody likes a liar!

For more information and FREE content, you can find
Andy and *The Super Twins* at:

www.andyslinger.com

www.facebook.com/andyslingeruk

www.instagram.com/andyslingeruk

https://twitter.com/andyslingeruk

About **Andy Slinger**

Andy is a 38-year-old single parent to identical twin boys Luke and Liam. Having spent most of his working life as a retail manager, he found that his real calling in life is writing kids' stories.

Since September 2019 he has worked his socks off to self-publish this book and hopes to soon become a full-time author, continuing *The Super Twins* series with book two.

"My aim is simple: to **engage, inspire** and **entertain** kids with my stories."

For further information about Andy and for exclusive content, sign up for his newsletter at:
www.andyslinger.com